Midnight Madness
at the Zoo

by Sherryn Craig

illustrated by Karen Jones

The sun goes down at eight o'clock.
The zoo begins to close.
The crowds are thinning out as all
the people leave for home.

The time cannot pass quick enough.
The game is still on tap.
It's Midnight Madness at the zoo—
no time to eat or nap.

The animals must warm up first
before they can roam free.
Some new officials take their place:
three zebras referee.

The trumpet of the elephants
calls players from their pens.
But for a game of basketball,
they'll need a group of ten.

One polar bear will start things off.
He dribbles back and forth.
He makes a couple layups when
a frog hops on the court.

Two players stay close to the net.
They play some one-on-one.
Just then a penguin darts inside—
her waddle's now a run.

Three ballers hustle down the lane.
They're going two-on-one.
Here comes a monkey swinging down
to join in all the fun.

Four players charge straight up the court.
They block and shoot and score.
But then a foul is called just as
a camel comes on board.

Five animals drive to the net—
three players against two.
One side is playing zone just when
a pig makes her debut.

Six players sprint to get the ball.
It's man-to-man defense.
That's when the ball goes out of bounds—
giraffe takes to offense.

Now **seven** ballers speed up play.
One side takes up the press.
A player goes to make a jam.
It's seal's turn to impress.

Eight players race to take the lead,
to open up the spread.
Next someone shoots a three just as
a mole drives on ahead.

Now **nine** are running up and down,
but wait, there is a steal.
A pass turns to an alley oop
as lion seals the deal.

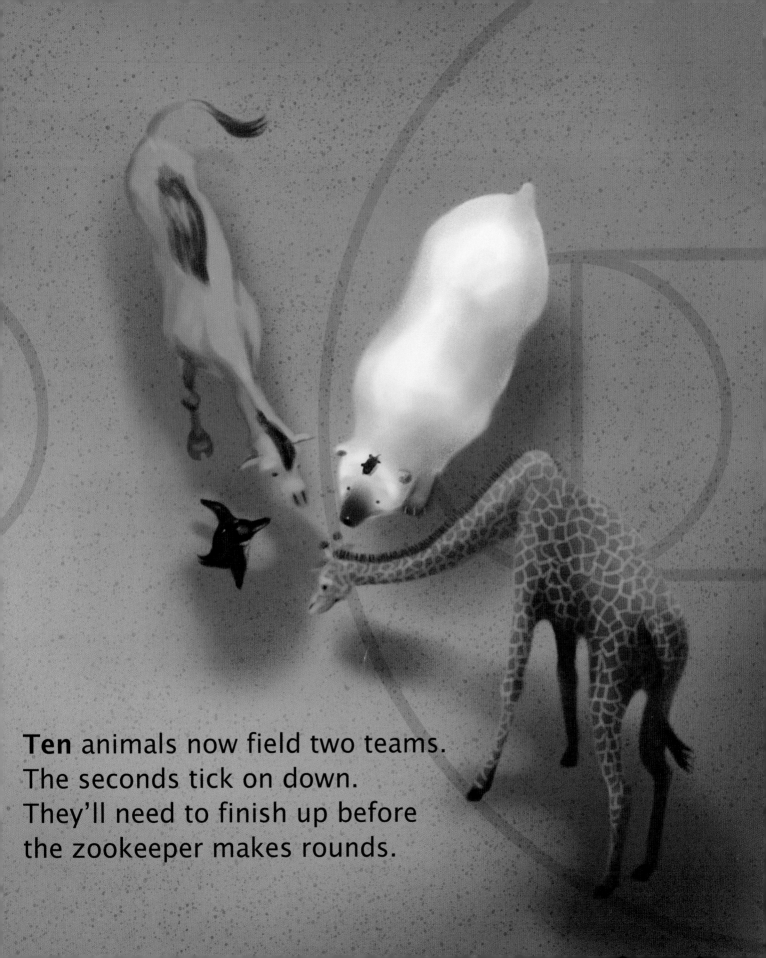

Ten animals now field two teams.
The seconds tick on down.
They'll need to finish up before
the zookeeper makes rounds.

They hear her whistle, then footsteps:
oh no, she's almost here!
They scramble back into their pens.
They're almost in the clear.

Just then they see her bending down—
she's scooping up a ball.
She shines her flashlight all around.
There's nothing strange at all.

She turns to leave and walks away.
They let go of their doubt.
Their secret is still safe for now.
They haven't been found out.

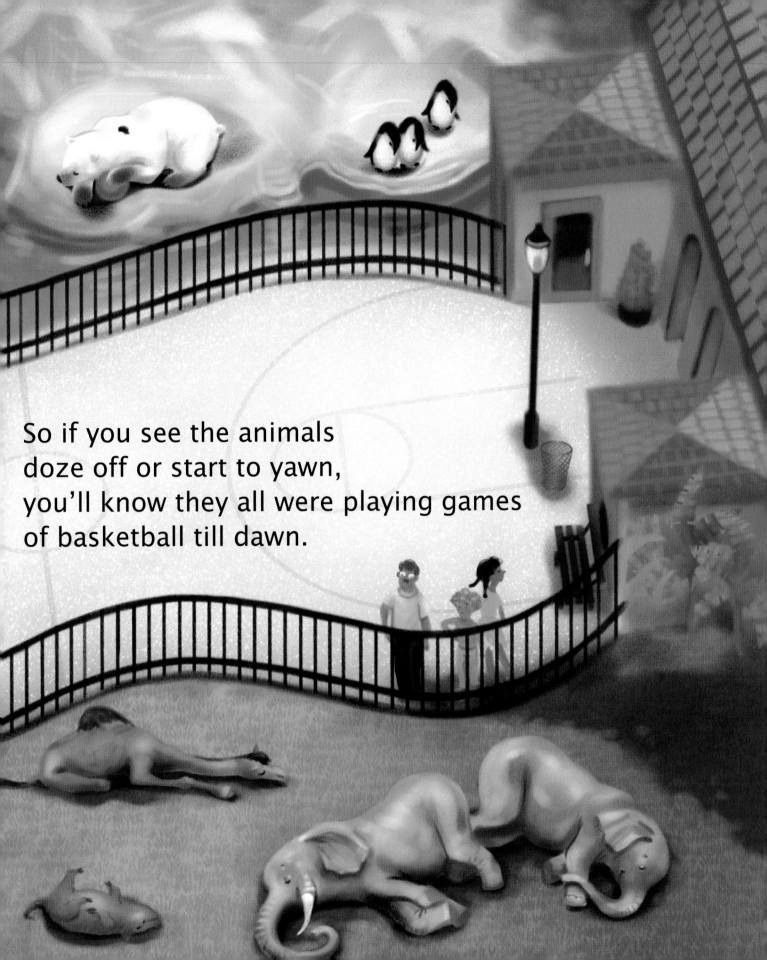

So if you see the animals
doze off or start to yawn,
you'll know they all were playing games
of basketball till dawn.

For Creative Minds

Basketball Vocabulary

alley oop: a player catches the ball in mid-air and dunks it

block: to knock the ball away from the basket

defense: the team without the basketball that tries to stop the other team from scoring

dribble: to bounce the basketball while walking or running on the basketball court

foul: when someone breaks the rules

layup: to shoot the ball into the basket from close up

make a jam: to jump up and throw (dunk) the ball straight down through the hoop

offense: the team with the basketball

open the spread: when the winning team scores more points to increase their lead

out of bounds: outside the basketball court

playing the zone: when a defensive player guards one area of the court

referee: a judge who makes sure both teams play by the rules

score: to win points

shoot: to aim and throw the ball toward the basket

shoot a three: to win three points with a single shot

steal: to take the ball away from another player

take up the press: to guard the offense the entire length of the basketball court

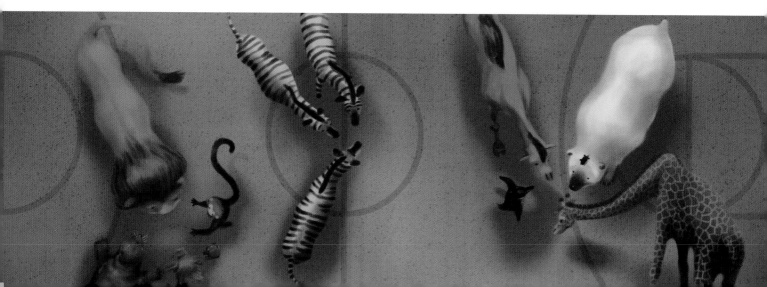

Ten in the Game

With ten players, there are many ways to divide up into two teams. Match each team on the left with a team on the right so that the two teams add up to ten players in the game.

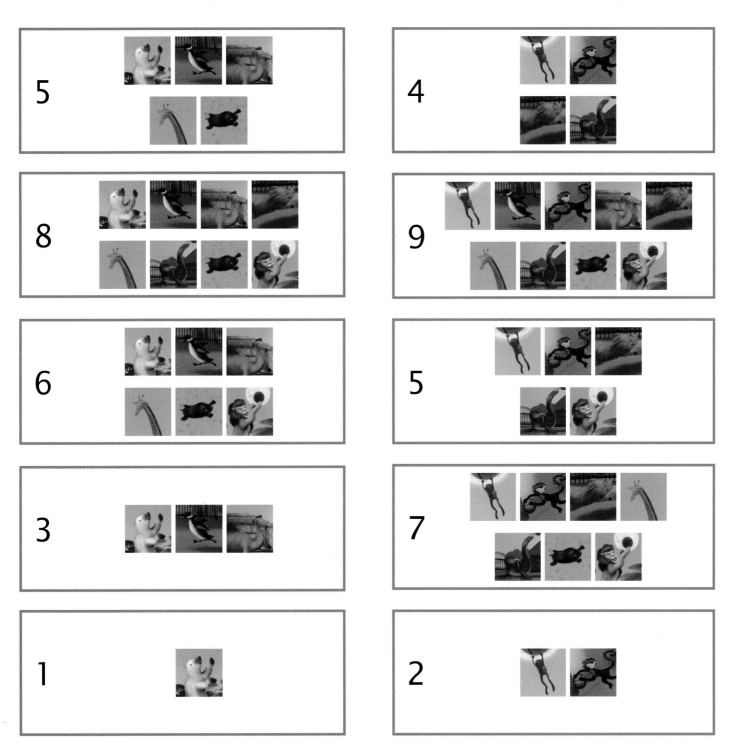

Answers: 5+5, 8+2, 6+4, 3+7, 1+9

Make it Count

In each of the scoreboards below, one team is winning (has the most points). How many points would the losing team need to score in order to tie the game (have the same number of points)?

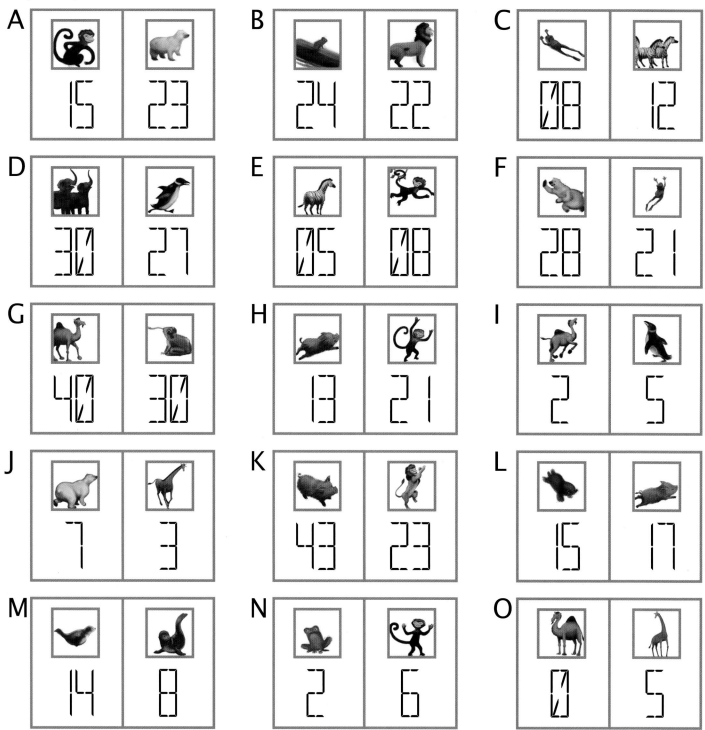

STEM Activity: Build a Basketball Hoop

Build a basketball hoop for yourself and your friends. Before you get started, plan out what you want to do. Think about what you want your basketball hoop to be like and what materials or tools you will need to build it.

- How big does the net have to be for the ball to pass through?
- What will you use for the net?
- How high off the ground do you want the net to be?
- What will you use to hold the net off the ground?
- How will you attach the net to its support?
- Do you want a backboard so you can bounce a ball into the net?
- What will you use for a backboard?
- How will you attach the backboard?
- Do you think your hoop could wobble or tip over if you bounce a ball off the backboard or against the net?
- How can you make your hoop sturdy enough to withstand the force of a ball hitting it?

Once you have planned your basketball hoop, gather your materials and tools. Be sure to check with an adult about any tools you need and use proper safety precautions. As you are working, you might find that something you planned doesn't work the way you wanted it to or you might think of a different way to meet your goal. It is okay to stop, think, and change your plans along the way.

Endangered Zoo Animals

Zoos are a place for people to see and learn about animals from all around the world. But they are also a place where people help animals that are in trouble. When an animal species is **endangered**, it means there are very few of those animals left in the world. Many of the animals in this story are endangered: elephants, polar bears, lions, and some species of penguins and monkeys.

Without help from people, these animals may disappear forever (become **extinct**). Zoos help endangered animals. This is called **conservation**. Zoos teach people about endangered animals and how humans can help them.

My coach . . . my cheerleader . . . my mom—Patricia Supon—for always believing in me. I love you!—SC

For Carter and Sydney—my heart and my soul.—KJ

Thanks to Bambi Godkin, Education Manager at Mill Mountain Zoo, for reviewing the accuracy of the zoo and conservation information, and to Derrick Pearson, sportscaster, for reviewing the basketball information in this book.

Library of Congress Cataloging-in-Publication Data

Names: Craig, Sherryn, author. | Jones, Karen, 1961- illustrator.
Title: Midnight madness at the zoo / by Sherryn Craig ; illustrated by Karen Jones.
Description: Mt. Pleasant, SC : Arbordale Publishing, [2016] | Summary: Between the time the crowds leave the zoo and the zookeeper makes her rounds, the animals come out for a rousing game of basketball.
Identifiers: LCCN 2015036425 (print) | LCCN 2015041620 (ebook) | ISBN 9781628557305 (english hardcover) | ISBN 9781628557374 (english pbk.) | ISBN 9781628557510 (english downloadable ebook) | ISBN 9781628557657 (english interactive dual-language ebook) | ISBN 9781628557442 (spanish pbk.) | ISBN 9781628557589 (spanish downloadable ebook) | ISBN 9781628557725 (spanish interactive dual-language ebook) | ISBN 9781628557510 (English Download) | ISBN 9781628557657 (Eng. Interactive) | ISBN 9781628557589 (Spanish Download) | ISBN 9781628557725 (Span. Interactive)
Subjects: | CYAC: Stories in rhyme. | Zoo animals--Fiction. | Basketball--Fiction. | Zoos--Fiction.
Classification: LCC PZ8.3.C (print) | LCC PZ8.3.C (ebook) | DDC [E]--dc23 LC record available at http://lccn.loc.gov/2015036425

Translated into Spanish: *Locura de medianoche en el zoológico*
Lexile® Level: AD 510
key phrases: add/subtract, anthropomorphic, counting, math: general, rhythm/rhyme

Manufactured in China, December 2015
This product conforms to CPSIA 2008
First Printing

Arbordale Publishing
Mt. Pleasant, SC 29464
www.ArbordalePublishing.com